World Team

TIM VYNER

RED FOX

For Joseph

WORLD TEAM
A RED FOX BOOK: 0 09 942758 3

First published in Great Britain by Red Fox,
an imprint of Random House Children's Books

This edition published 2002

5 7 9 10 8 6 4

© Tim Vyner 2002

Red Fox Books are published by Random House Children's Books,
61-63 Uxbridge Road, London W5 5SA,
a division of The Random House Group Ltd,
in Australia by Random House Australia (Pty) Ltd,
20 Alfred Street, Milsons Point, Sydney, NSW 2061, Australia,
in New Zealand by Random House New Zealand Ltd,
18 Poland Road, Glenfield, Auckland 10, New Zealand,
and in South Africa by Random House (Pty) Ltd,
Endulini, 5A Jubilee Road, Parktown 2193, South Africa

THE RANDOM HOUSE GROUP Limited Reg. No. 954009
www.kidsatrandomhouse.co.uk

A CIP catalogue record for this book
is available from the British Library

Printed in Singapore by Tien Wah Press (PTE) Ltd

Note: world times are offset from Greenwich Mean Time

One big round world, one small round ball.
Right now there are more children than you can
possibly imagine playing football.

At this very moment, Joe is playing football outside
his school. He practises every afternoon.

"And when I grow up, I'm going to be a professional!"

At the same time, Gianni skips along the street never taking his eyes off the ball.

"This header for a golden goal," he imagines.

Meanwhile, the sun comes up in Rio de Janeiro and Tico is also dreaming of World Cup glory.

"When I grow up, I am going to have my own boots!"

In Calcutta, the sun is going down as Ravi
practises against a wall. He has been selling ice cream

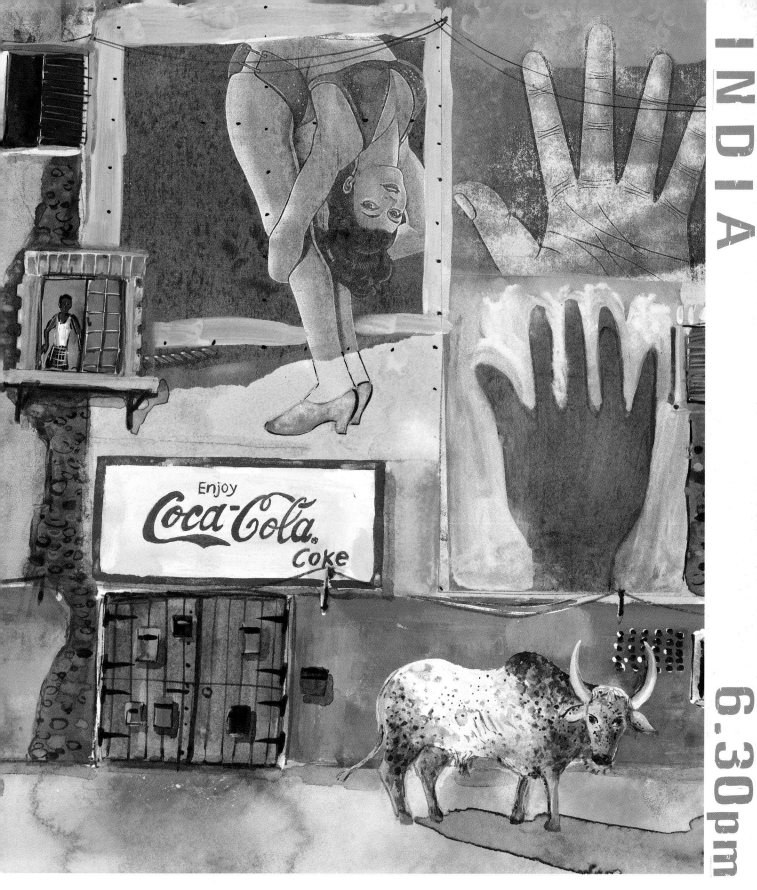

all day and has saved the last one for himself.
"Today was hot; it will be cooler in the evening shade."

Lucy darts in and out of the morning shadows in New York as she makes her way to school after soccer training.

"I've been running up and down the pitch, and scoring goals," she says, "and now I'm thirsty!"

It is the hottest time of day when Sami buys a drink
from the ice seller in the ruined stadium.

"Imagine what this place was like in the old days," he says.
"And think of all the people inside."

Meanwhile, Pablo is standing outside the new Barcelona stadium just before the big game.

It is his birthday and he is going to see his
first ever live match.
"It's amazing!" he exclaims.

Thousands of miles away, Suki is watching
the same match in his bedroom.

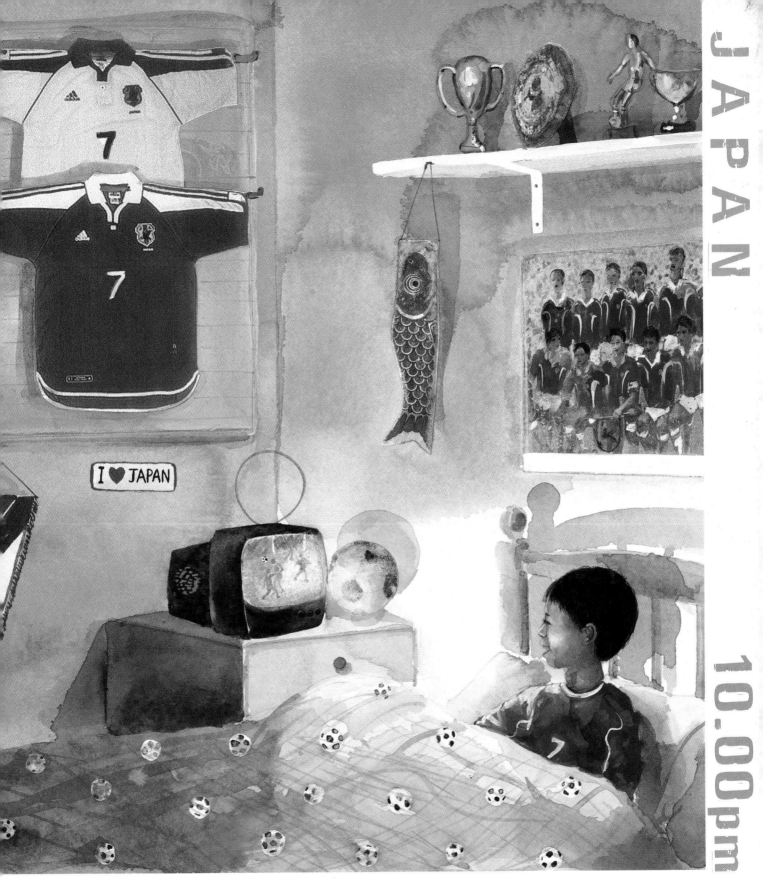

"I'm allowed to stay up for the live games!"
he says excitedly.

And in the hot, dry outback Mickie cannot sleep.
"Some nights it is just *too* hot to sleep," he thinks

as he listens to the same game on the radio.

Carlos turns the radio on and stretches out. He has woken up at first light because he is going fishing with his father. But before they set off he grabs a ball.

"I have to practise my shooting now because it will be too hot and dusty when we get back," he says.

The afternoon sun blazes over the pitch where Zachary plays.
Swirling dust burns his eyes.

"The sun feels good on my back, but one day I will play on a grass pitch where my eyes won't itch," he thinks. "It will be easier when the rains come," he adds.

Henri and his team have been playing for more than an hour.
"Allez tout le monde! Just five more minutes.

Next goal wins the World Cup," he shouts.

In the hot sunshine,
Nelson organises his own players.

"One day I will be in charge of a real team," he thinks to himself. "And one day we will win the World Cup."

Joe, Gianni, Tico, Ravi, Lucy, Sami, Pablo, Suki, Mickie, Carlos, Zachary, Henri and Nelson, and millions like them, are all playing football together.

And at the same time, they share the same dream -
of winning the World Cup.

One small round world, one big round ball.
And right now there are more children around the world
playing football than you can possibly imagine.